Shadows of Retribution

By Dez'Neil Jones

Genre: Horror/Thriller

Table of Contents

1. Chapter 1: The Gathering Storm
2. Chapter 2: Echoes of the Past
3. Chapter 3: The Unraveling
4. Chapter 4: The Confrontation
5. Chapter 5: Whispers in the Dark
6. Chapter 6: The Echoes of Vengeance
7. Chapter 7: Confronting the Shadows
8. Chapter 8: The Breaking Dawn
9. Chapter 9: The Heart of Darkness
10. Chapter 10: The Dawn of a New Day
11. Chapter 11: The Shattering
12. Chapter 12: The Final Escape

Premise:

In the quiet halls of Crestwood University, a former high school outcast named Lucas finds himself at a crossroads. Years of relentless bullying have left him scarred and vengeful. As he begins his college journey, he discovers a dark power within himself that he never knew existed, and he becomes determined to exact revenge on those who tormented him.

Act One: The Return
Chapter 1: The Gathering Storm

The Whitmore estate, an imposing relic of a long-forgotten era, towered on the outskirts of the small town of Eldridge Hollow. Its jagged spires clawed at the darkening sky, creating an unsettling silhouette against the backdrop of the encroaching dusk. As Alex maneuvered the winding driveway, an undeniable sense of foreboding enveloped the group of college students crammed into his vehicle. The mansion, cloaked in shadows and draped in neglect, appeared as if it had been abandoned by both time and the vitality of the living.

"Well, we're really doing this, huh?" Mia questioned, her skepticism evident as she squinted at the foreboding structure that loomed before them.

"Come on, it's going to be an adventure!" Alex replied, his enthusiasm unwavering despite the oppressive atmosphere surrounding them. He had always been the fearless leader, eager to dive headfirst into the unknown and embrace whatever mysteries lay ahead.

Jordan, the group's resident history enthusiast, leaned forward, his eyes alight with curiosity. "This house is steeped in dark legends. The Whitmore family was rumored to have engaged in some rather sinister practices. They say it's haunted by the spirits of its former inhabitants."

"Fantastic, just what we need," Lila muttered, her grip tightening around her backpack as they parked and stepped out into the biting evening air, which felt thick with anticipation.

As they approached the grand entrance, the massive front door creaked open as if inviting them inside—or perhaps issuing a warning to turn back. The interior was just as unsettling as the exterior suggested. Dust motes danced in the dim light, and the air hung heavy with the musty scent of decay and neglect.

They wandered through the ground floor, each room revealing remnants of a once-vibrant life: faded photographs trapped in cracked frames, shrouded furniture cloaked in white sheets, and an eerie silence that seemed to pulse with a life of its own.

Suddenly, a loud bang reverberated from the upper floors, causing their hearts to leap in their chests. "Probably just the house settling," Alex said, attempting to inject humor into the situation, but the tremor in his voice betrayed his own unease.

As night enveloped them like a thick blanket, the group settled in for the evening, yet the oppressive atmosphere clung to them like a second skin. Shadows crept along the walls, whispering secrets that only the old mansion could divulge, leaving the students feeling as though they were being watched by unseen eyes.

Chapter 2: Echoes of the Past

The following day dawned cold and gray, the sun struggling to pierce the heavy clouds that loomed overhead. The group gathered in the dimly lit living room, the flickering fire casting dancing shadows that twisted across their faces. Lila, ever the superstitious one, suggested they share ghost stories to lighten the mood.

As laughter filled the room, Mia's curiosity drew her to a dusty bookshelf in the corner. Her fingers brushed against a weathered leather-bound journal, its spine cracked and brittle with age. With a sense of trepidation, she pulled it down and began to read aloud.

The journal belonged to Eliza Whitmore, the last surviving member of the family. Her entries were a haunting chronicle of despair, detailing a harrowing descent into madness, betrayal, and an insatiable thirst for vengeance that seemed to linger even beyond death. "This is seriously creepy," Mia remarked, her voice quaking as she recounted the tragic fates that befell the Whitmores—each death more gruesome than the last.

As she read, a sudden gust of wind howled through the creaking windows, extinguishing the flickering candles and plunging the room into an unsettling darkness. Panic surged through the group as they scrambled for their phones, the glow of their screens casting eerie silhouettes against the walls.

"Maybe we should just leave," Lila suggested, her voice a mere whisper, trembling with fear.

"No way! We're not leaving now," Alex insisted, though uncertainty clouded his tone. "We need to uncover the truth about this place."

As they huddled together, the sensation of being watched intensified, each creak of the house echoing their unspoken fears and leaving them questioning the wisdom of their decision to remain.

Chapter 3: The Unraveling

The morning sun struggled to break through the thick cover of clouds, casting a dreary pall over the estate. Determined to delve deeper into the Whitmore legacy, the group ventured outside, and their breath visible in the crisp, biting air.

As they explored the grounds, they stumbled upon a hidden graveyard, the tombstones standing like silent sentinels amidst the overgrown grass. Each name etched into the stones sent shivers down their spines, the dates revealing a tragic history that weighed heavily on their hearts.

"Why are all the graves so close together?" Jordan pondered, his brow furrowing as he examined a particularly weathered headstone. "It's almost as if they were hastily buried."

While Lila traced her fingers over the names, a chilling sensation coursed through her. "We shouldn't be here. It feels like we're disturbing something that should remain undisturbed."

But Alex remained resolute, his determination unwavering. "We need to know what really happened. There must be more to this story."

As they ventured deeper into the grounds, strange occurrences began to escalate. Shadows flitted just out of sight, and whispers seemed to float on the wind, chilling them to the bone.

That night, Lila awoke from a nightmare, drenched in sweat. She had seen a shadowy figure standing at the foot of her bed, its eyes burning with an insatiable hunger. When she shared her horrifying vision with the group, fear rippled through them, fracturing their fragile unity.

Chapter 4: The Confrontation

With the atmosphere thickening, the group attempted to regroup, but the tension in the air was almost suffocating. Voices rose in heated debate as they gathered in the living room, when suddenly, one of their own—Jordan—vanished without a trace.

"Where could he have gone?" Mia asked, panic gnawing at her insides as they frantically searched the mansion.

"Maybe he stepped outside for a moment," Alex suggested, though uncertainty clouded his tone, a hint of desperation creeping into his voice.

As they split up to search the sprawling estate, each member confronted the encroaching darkness alone. Lila wandered into a room filled with mirrors, her reflection twisting and warping until she barely recognized herself, the images mocking her with their distorted faces.

Mia found herself back in the library, the journal still open on the table, its pages fluttering as though caught in an unseen breeze. The whispers grew louder, echoing Eliza's desperate cries for aid, drawing her deeper into the haunting narrative of the past.

Meanwhile, Alex ventured into the basement, where a chill wrapped around him like an icy shroud. Shadows danced along the walls, and a low growl reverberated through the air, sending shivers down his spine. He felt the presence before he saw it—a dark figure lurking in the corner, its eyes glowing with malevolent intent.

As the group reconvened, panic etched on their faces, Lila screamed, "We have to get out of here now!" But it was too late. The shadows had awakened, and the darkness was hungry for retribution.

Act Two: The Unraveling Shadows
Chapter 5: Whispers in the Dark

The atmosphere within the hallowed walls of the Whitmore estate grew increasingly oppressive as the sun sank beneath the horizon, casting elongated shadows that stretched like skeletal fingers across the ancient walls. The group huddled together in the dimly lit living room, their hearts pounding with an unsettling mix of fear and disbelief as they grappled with the shocking transformation of Jordan. He stood apart from them, a mere husk of the vibrant friend they once knew, his gaze vacant, and his eyes clouded with a sinister, otherworldly light.

"Jordan, can you hear us?" Mia called out hesitantly, her voice tinged with anxiety as she took a cautious step forward. But he merely stared blankly, as if lost in a realm far removed from their reality.

"What if he's... possessed?" Lila whispered, her voice quivering with trepidation as she wrapped her arms tightly around herself, seeking comfort in her own warmth amidst the growing chill.

"I don't know what's happening, but we can't just abandon him like this," Alex asserted, his face set with determination. "We need to find a way to help him, no matter what it takes."

With heavy hearts burdened by dread, the group made the decision to delve deeper into the mansion, hoping to uncover the elusive answers that lay hidden within its dark corners. As they ventured down a narrow, dimly lit hallway, the air grew noticeably colder, and the walls seemed to close in around them, suffocating their resolve. Flickering lights illuminated unsettling portraits of the Whitmore family, their painted eyes appearing to follow the group with an accusatory, almost sentient gaze.

In the kitchen, they stumbled upon a concealed trapdoor beneath a tattered rug, its presence almost mocking in the face of their despair. Heart pounding with a mixture of fear and excitement, Alex knelt to pry it open, revealing a rickety staircase that spiraled down into an oppressive darkness. "This could be where they kept their darkest secrets," he proposed, glancing back at the others, who shared a mix of fear and curiosity. "We have to check it out."

Steeling themselves against the unknown, they descended the creaking stairs, the air growing thicker and more suffocating with every step they took. At the bottom, they entered a dimly lit cellar filled with old crates and dusty artifacts that bore witness to the passage of time. A chill ran down their spines as they stumbled upon a large, ornate mirror draped in a tattered cloth, its presence commanding and foreboding.

"What's this?" Mia asked, her curiosity piqued as she reached to pull the cloth away. The mirror's surface shimmered, revealing distorted reflections that twisted and writhed as if alive, tantalizing and terrifying all at once.

Suddenly, an ominous voice echoed through the cellar—a low, guttural growl that resonated deep within their chests, reverberating with an unsettling vibration. "Leave… now…"

The group froze, terror gripping their hearts as they turned to flee, but the cellar door slammed shut with a thunderous bang, trapping them inside the suffocating darkness. Panic surged through their veins, and they pounded desperately on the door, but it remained steadfastly closed, resisting their frantic efforts to escape.

Chapter 6: The Echoes of Vengeance

As fear escalated, the group looked at one another, their expressions a mix of dread and determination. "What do we do now?" Lila cried, her voice rising in pitch as anxiety threatened to overwhelm her.

"Stay calm! We need to think clearly," Alex urged, his mind racing to formulate a plan. He scanned the room, his gaze landing on the mirror that had captivated those moments before. "Maybe we can use it somehow to our advantage."

As they gathered around the ornate mirror, its surface flickered with unsettling images—visions of the Whitmore family in their final, anguished moments, their faces twisted in terror as shadows enveloped them like a shroud of despair. The echoes of their screams resonated within the very walls of the cellar, filling the air with a heavy sense of desperation and hopelessness.

Mia stepped closer, entranced by the haunting visions. "They were victims, just like us," she murmured, her heart aching for the souls trapped in the mirror's reflection. "They're stuck here, just like Jordan is."

Suddenly, the mirror rippled violently, and a figure emerged—a ghostly apparition of Eliza Whitmore, her eyes brimming with a potent mix of sorrow and rage. "You must help me," she implored, her voice a haunting melody laced with desperation. "The darkness that consumed my family seeks to claim you as well!"

"What do we need to do?" Alex asked, determination igniting within him as he stepped closer to the spirit, eager to find a way to save their friend and the trapped souls.

"Free us from the curse that binds our souls," Eliza replied, her form flickering like a candle in a tempest. "You must confront the darkness that dwells within these walls. Only then can you save your friend and yourselves."

With a surge of resolve, they agreed to confront the malevolent force that haunted the estate. Eliza's spirit guided them, revealing the hidden history of the Whitmore family and the dark rituals that had ensnared them for eternity.

As the mirror shimmered once more, they glimpsed fragments of the past—rituals performed in secrecy, pacts made with dark entities, and the tragic downfall of the Whitmore family. Each revelation deepened their understanding of the curse that bound Jordan and the souls of the Whitmores to the estate, illuminating the path they needed to take to break the cycle of torment that had haunted them for generations.

Chapter 7: Confronting the Shadows

With their newfound purpose, the group emerged from the cellar, determined to confront the encroaching darkness that had taken hold of Jordan. The air felt charged with tension as they regrouped in the living room, the flickering lights casting unsettling shadows across the room's every corner.

"Jordan, we're going to bring you back," Alex declared, his voice steady despite the turmoil within him. "We need you to fight this. We're not giving up on you, not now."

But Jordan's gaze remained empty, his body seemingly under the thrall of some unseen force. As they closed their eyes, focusing on the bond they shared, they whispered memories of their friendship—laughter shared, adventures undertaken, and moments of vulnerability that had woven their lives together.

Suddenly, a dark wind swept through the room, extinguishing the flickering lights and plunging them into an oppressive darkness. A chilling voice echoed through the air, reverberating with malice. "You cannot save him. He belongs to me now!"

The group huddled together, their fear palpable, yet their resolve began to solidify. "Stay close!" Mia shouted, her voice rising strong amid the chaos.

With the shadows swirling around them like a tempest, they summoned their courage and stepped forward, ready to confront the very essence of the darkness that sought to destroy them. Eliza's spirit appeared beside them, her presence a beacon of hope amid the encroaching despair. "Together, you can break the curse," she urged, her voice rising above the din of fear. "You must confront the shadows that have taken your friend."

Understanding that they needed to face the very embodiment of the darkness, they followed Eliza's guidance, moving toward the heart of the mansion where the malevolence seemed to be concentrated. As they ventured deeper into the estate, the air thickened with an almost palpable malice, the shadows stretching and twisting like serpents poised to strike.

Entering a grand ballroom, they were met with a disquieting sight—the floor was littered with remnants of the past: shattered mirrors, broken furniture, and dark stains that told stories of anguish and despair. In the center of the room stood Jordan, his body surrounded by swirling shadows that pulsed with dark energy, threatening to consume him entirely.

"Jordan!" Lila cried, reaching out to him, desperation flooding her voice. "Fight it! We're here for you!"

But the shadows coiled around him like a vice, and a chilling laugh filled the room. "He is mine!" the voice boomed, drowning out their pleas, resonating with a dreadful finality.

With Eliza's spirit guiding them, they formed a protective circle around Jordan, channeling their energy and love into a brilliant, radiant light. "We won't abandon you!" Alex shouted, his voice resonating with unyielding strength.

As the light intensified, the shadows recoiled, hissing and writhing as they fought against the illumination. Jordan's eyes flickered, a glimmer of recognition breaking through the darkness, the bond of friendship piercing the veil that had shrouded him.

Chapter 8: The Breaking Dawn

The battle between light and shadow raged within the grand ballroom, the air crackling with energy as the group fought to reclaim their friend from the clutches of darkness. With each pulse of their collective resolve, the shadows shrank back, revealing glimpses of Jordan beneath the oppressive weight.

"Come back to us, Jordan!" Mia cried, her voice filled with determination and hope. "We believe in you!"

As the light enveloped Jordan, memories flooded his mind—shared laughter, whispered secrets, and the unbreakable bond of friendship that had withstood the tests of time. The malevolent voice screamed in fury, attempting to drown out their encouragement.

"No! He belongs to me! He will never escape!"

But the bond forged through love and shared experiences proved stronger than the darkness. With one final surge of energy, the group channeled their love into a blinding light that exploded forth, shattering the shadows that encircled Jordan.

The darkness writhed and twisted, shrieking in agony as it dissipated into nothingness. Jordan collapsed onto the floor, gasping for breath as the shadows finally released their hold.

"Jordan!" Lila rushed to his side, cradling his head in her lap, tears of relief streaming down her cheeks. "Are you okay?"

He blinked, confusion clouding his gaze before clarity returned, the warmth of their friendship seeping into his very core. "What happened? I… I felt lost," he murmured, his voice trembling with the remnants of fear.

"We fought for you," Alex explained, relief flooding his voice. "Eliza helped us. Now we need to finish this and free her family from the curse that has haunted this place for so long."

As they regrouped, Eliza's spirit materialized once more, her ethereal form shimmering with gratitude and a sense of peace. "Thank you," she whispered, her voice a haunting melody filled with appreciation. "You have freed my family from the chains of darkness. But there is still work to be done."

With renewed purpose, the group followed Eliza, their hearts racing as they prepared to confront the final remnants of the curse that had plagued the estate for generations. As they moved toward the heart of the mansion, each step echoed with the promise of liberation and the hope of dawn breaking over the shadows, eager to banish the darkness that had long held sway over the Whitmore estate.

Act Three: The Reckoning of Shadows
Chapter 9: The Heart of Darkness

The air was charged with an electric anticipation as the group plunged deeper into the ominous depths of the Whitmore estate, compelled by an urgent need to confront the malevolent force that had long haunted its darkened corridors. With Eliza's spectral presence guiding them, they navigated the labyrinthine passages, the flickering candles casting quivering shadows that danced ominously on the ancient stone walls. Each step felt heavier, as if the weight of the estate's dark history pressed down upon them, threatening to crush their resolve and extinguish their hope.

As they approached a pair of imposing double doors at the end of a long, dimly lit hallway, the atmosphere thickened, and an unsettling chill enveloped them. The doors were ornately carved, adorned with ominous depictions of the Whitmore family engaged in what appeared to be a dark ritual—faces twisted in agony, hands raised in supplication to a shadowy figure looming above. "This must be it," Alex said, his voice barely above a whisper, laced with both dread and determination. "This is where the heart of the darkness lies."

Mia nodded, her heart racing as she reached for the cold metal handle, feeling a jolt of fear course through her. "Together," she urged, glancing at her friends, their apprehensive expressions mirroring her own. "We can do this."

With a collective breath, they pushed the doors open, revealing a vast chamber bathed in an eerie, dim light. The air was thick with the scent of damp earth, decay, and something far more sinister—a palpable presence that made their skin crawl. At the center of the room stood a large altar, draped in dark velvet and surrounded by flickering candles that cast ghostly shadows across the stone floor.

Eliza's spirit materialized beside them, her translucent figure glowing softly in the dim light. "This is where my family performed their rituals," she explained, her voice echoing in the vast space. "This is where the darkness was summoned, where the bonds were forged that now ensnare us."

As the group stepped further into the chamber, they noticed intricate inscriptions etched into the stone walls—arcane symbols and incantations that seemed to pulse with a life of their own, whispering secrets of power and despair. "These are the markings of the ritual that bound my family to this place," Eliza said, her expression a mixture of sorrow and determination. "You must break this binding spell if you are to free us all."

Jordan, still recovering from the shadows that had claimed him, looked around, his brow furrowed with concern. "How do we break it?" he asked, anxiety creeping into his voice.

"You must confront the entity that resides here," Eliza replied, her voice steady yet filled with urgency.

"It feeds on fear and despair. Only by facing it together can you sever the ties that bind us."

As Eliza spoke, the air grew colder, and a low growl resonated from the shadows, echoing ominously throughout the chamber. "You dare to challenge me?" a voice boomed, thick with malice and contempt. The shadows at the periphery of the room began to coalesce, forming a dark figure that loomed larger than life, its eyes glowing with a malevolent fire that pierced the dimness.

"We are here to end your reign!" Alex shouted, his voice ringing with defiance, though doubt gnawed at the edges of his confidence.

The entity laughed, a sound that sent chills racing down their spines, reverberating through the chamber like thunder. "You think you can defeat me? I am the darkness that dwells in every heart, the despair that lingers in every soul. You are but children playing at bravery, unprepared for the true depths of fear."

Chapter 10: The Dance of Shadows

"Do not listen to its lies!" Eliza urged, her voice rising above the cacophony of shadows. "You have the power to overcome it! Remember your strength, your bond!"

The group stood firm, each member drawing strength from the memories they shared—moments of joy, laughter, and trust that had woven their lives together through trials and tribulations. "We won't let you take us down!" Mia shouted, stepping forward as a wave of determination surged within her.

The entity recoiled slightly, its form flickering as if it were unsure of its hold on them. "What is this?" it hissed, its voice dripping with disdain and disbelief. "Your light is weak; it cannot hope to extinguish me."

With newfound resolve, the group joined hands, forming a protective circle around the altar. They began to chant the incantations inscribed on the walls, their voices rising in a harmonious union as they recalled the warmth of their shared memories—friendship, courage, and love. The air around them shimmered with energy, and the candles on the altar flared to life, illuminating the chamber with a brilliant glow that chased away the shadows.

The entity screeched, rage contorting its features as it realized the power of their unity. "You think you can banish me with mere words? I will consume you all!" it bellowed, its voice echoing with fury.

As the chanting grew louder, the shadows writhed, and the entity lunged forward, dark tendrils reaching for the group, eager to ensnare them in its grasp. But they stood firm, their connection strengthening as they poured their emotions into the incantation. The room shimmered with light, pushing back against the encroaching darkness.

Suddenly, a powerful wave of energy surged from the altar, cascading over the group like a tidal wave. They felt an overwhelming force pulling them apart, threatening to sever their bond. "Hold on to each other!" Alex shouted, his voice barely audible above the din. "We can do this together!"

With every ounce of strength they possessed, the group pressed forward, their voices echoing through the chamber like a chorus of defiance. The light intensified, pushing the darkness back, but the entity fought with ferocity, its tendrils striking out and threatening to ensnare them.

In a moment of desperation, Lila closed her eyes, recalling the happiest memory she had—her first camping trip with her friends, laughing around a campfire as stars twinkled overhead. The warmth of that memory filled her heart, and she poured it into the chant. "We are more than just friends; we are family!"

Her words resonated, igniting a spark in the others. One by one, they began to share their own memories, their voices intertwining, creating a tapestry of light that began to push back the shadows and illuminate the chamber.

Chapter 11: The Shattering

As they chanted with renewed vigor, the energy in the chamber swirled around them, forming a brilliant vortex of light that clashed against the advancing darkness. The entity roared in fury, its form becoming increasingly unstable as it struggled against the light. "No! You cannot defeat me! I am eternal!" it bellowed, but doubt began to creep into its voice, fear evident in its tone.

The group felt a surge of strength as their bond intensified, and the light began to coalesce into a singular, blinding force that radiated warmth and hope. "We are not afraid of you!" Jordan shouted, his voice clear and firm as he stepped forward, embodying their collective courage. "You will no longer control us!"

With one final push, they directed all of their energy into a single, powerful incantation. The light exploded outward, enveloping the entity and illuminating the entire chamber in a radiant glow. The walls trembled, and the very foundation of the estate shook as the shadows writhed in agony.

"NO!" the entity screamed, its voice filled with rage and panic. "I will not be denied!"

But the light was relentless, shattering the darkness and breaking the entity's hold on the mansion. The shadows recoiled, dissipating into the ether as the group felt a wave of energy crash over them. They stood together, hands clasped tightly, the warmth of their connection radiating through the chaos.

As the entity disintegrated, a deafening silence fell over the chamber, broken only by the soft flicker of the candles. The air felt lighter, and the oppressive weight that had hung over the estate began to lift, replaced by a sense of victory.

"Is it over?" Lila whispered, her heart racing as she looked around, half-expecting the darkness to return and engulf them once more.

Eliza's spirit appeared before them, her expression serene and filled with gratitude. "You have done it. You have freed my family and defeated the darkness that plagued this estate. I am forever grateful."

However, just as they began to breathe a sigh of relief, a low rumble echoed through the chamber, and the ground beneath them began to shake violently. "What's happening?" Mia cried, her eyes wide with fear, panic rising within her.

The walls of the chamber trembled, and cracks began to form, snaking across the stone like veins. "We need to get out of here!" Alex shouted, urgency lacing his voice, the reality of their situation sinking in.

Chapter 12: The Final Escape

The group turned to flee, but the trembling ground made it difficult to maintain their footing. "Hurry!" Jordan urged, racing toward the exit as the walls seemed to close in around them. They sprinted through the chamber, dodging falling debris as the very structure of the mansion threatened to collapse.

As they reached the staircase, a massive crack erupted in the wall beside them, sending a shower of bricks tumbling down like rain. "Move!" Alex yelled, shoving Lila ahead of him as they barreled down the stairs, each step vibrating beneath them with the force of the mansion's impending collapse.

They burst into the main hall, the front door in sight, but the ground shook violently, and the ceiling began to cave in around them. "Run!" Mia screamed, sprinting toward the exit as they heard the ominous sound of wood splintering above them.

They dashed through the front door just as the house gave one final, agonizing groan. The ground cracked open, and the mansion began to implode, sending a cloud of dust and debris soaring into the sky. The darkness that had haunted the estate for centuries was finally gone.

But as they caught their breath, a chilling wind whipped across the grounds, and a voice echoed in the distance, filled with rage and despair. "You may have defeated me, but this is not over. I will return… and I will have my revenge!"

The group exchanged terrified glances, the weight of the entity's threat hanging in the air like a dark cloud. They had won a battle, but the war against the shadows was far from over.

As the dust settled and the first light of dawn broke over the horizon, they realized that their journey was only just beginning, and the shadows of the past would continue to loom large over their lives. Unbeknownst to them, the darkness was not merely a force of nature, but a cunning entity that would bide its time, waiting for the perfect moment to strike again.

And as they stood together in the aftermath of the collapse, a sense of foreboding crept into their hearts—an unsettling realization that their lives would never be the same again, forever marked by the shadows that lurked just beyond the veil of their perception.

Made in the USA
Columbia, SC
16 May 2025